The
Julian
Stories

The Julian Stories

Ann Cameron

Illustrated by Jamie Smith

Tamarind

THE JULIAN STORIES
A TAMARIND BOOK 978 1 848 53084 3

First published in the USA in 1981 as *The Stories Julian Tells* by Pantheon Books
First published in Great Britain in 1982 by Victor Gollancz Ltd

This edition published by Tamarind Books,
an imprint of Random House Children's Publishers UK
A Random House Group Company

Tamarind edition published 2013

5 7 9 10 8 6

Text copyright © Ann Cameron, 1981
Illustrations © Jamie Smith, 2013

The right of Ann Cameron and Jamie Smith to be identified as the author and
illustrator of this work has been asserted in accordance with the
Copyright, Designs and Patents Act 1988.

The Random House Group Limited supports The Forest Stewardship
Council® (FSC®), the leading international forest-certification organisation.
Our books carrying the FSC label are printed on FSC®-certified paper.
FSC is the only forest-certification scheme supported by the leading
environmental organisations, including Greenpeace. Our
paper procurement policy can be found at
www.randomhouse.co.uk/environment

MIX
Paper from
responsible sources
FSC® C016897

Set in Bembo MT

Tamarind Books are published by Random House Children's Publishers UK,
61–63 Uxbridge Road, London W5 5SA

www.tamarindbooks.co.uk
www.randomhousechildrens.co.uk
www.randomhouse.co.uk

Addresses for companies within The Random House Group Limited can be found at:
www.randomhouse.co.uk/offices.htm

THE RANDOM HOUSE GROUP Limited Reg. No. 954009

A CIP catalogue record for this book is available from the British Library.

Printed and bound in Great Britain by Clays Ltd, St Ives PLC

To Frances Foster and Monica Klein
with gratitude

Contents

The Pudding
Like a
Night on the Sea

"I'm going to make something special for your mother," my father said.

My mother was out shopping. My father was in the kitchen looking at the pots and the pans and the jars of this and that.

"What are you going to make?" I said.

"A pudding," he said.

My father is a big man with wild black hair. When he laughs, the sun laughs in the windowpanes. When he thinks, you can almost see his thoughts sitting on all the tables and chairs. When he is angry, me and my little brother Huey shiver to the bottom of our shoes.

"What kind of pudding will you make?" Huey said.

"A wonderful pudding," my father said. "It will taste like a whole raft of lemons. It will taste like a night on the sea."

Then he took down a knife and sliced five lemons in half. He squeezed the first one. Juice squirted in my eye.

"Stand back!" he said, and squeezed again. The seeds flew out on the floor. "Pick up those seeds, Huey!" he said.

Huey took the broom and swept them up.

My father cracked some eggs and put the yolks in a pan and the whites in a

bowl. He rolled up his sleeves and pushed back his hair and beat up the yolks. "Sugar, Julian!" he said, and I poured in the sugar.

He went on beating. Then he put in lemon juice and cream and set the pan on the stove. The pudding bubbled and he stirred it fast. Cream splashed on the stove.

"Wipe that up, Huey!" he said.

Huey did.

It was hot by the stove. My father loosened his collar and pushed at his sleeves. The stuff in the pan was getting thicker and thicker. He held the beater up high in the air. "Just right!" he said, and sniffed in the smell of the pudding.

He whipped the egg whites and mixed them into the pudding. The pudding looked softer and lighter than air.

"Done!" he said. He washed all the pots, splashing water on the floor, and wiped the counter so fast his hair made circles around his head.

"Perfect!" he said. "Now I'm going to take a nap. If something important happens, bother me. If nothing important happens, don't bother me. And − the pudding is for your mother. Leave the pudding alone!"

He went to the living room and was asleep in a minute, sitting straight up in his chair.

Huey and I guarded the pudding.

"Oh, it's a wonderful pudding," Huey said.

"With waves on the top like the ocean," I said.

"I wonder how it tastes," Huey said.

"Leave the pudding alone," I said.

"If I just put my finger in – there – I'll know how it tastes," Huey said.

And he did it.

"You did it!" I said. "How does it taste?"

"It tastes like a whole raft of lemons," he said. "It tastes like a night on the sea."

"You've made a hole in the pudding!" I said. "But since *you* did it, *I'll* have a taste." And it tasted like a whole night of lemons. It tasted like floating at sea.

"It's such a big pudding," Huey said. "It can't hurt to have a little more."

"Since you took more, I'll have more," I said.

"That was a bigger lick than I took!" Huey said. "I'm going to have more again."

"Whoops!" I said.

"You put in your whole hand!" Huey said. "Look at the pudding you spilled on the floor!"

"I am going to clean it up," I said. And I took the rag from the sink.

"That's not really clean," Huey said.

"It's the best I can do," I said.

"Look at the pudding!" Huey said.

It looked like craters on the moon. "We have to smooth this over," I said. "So it looks the way it did before! Let's get spoons."

And we evened the top of the pudding with spoons, and while we evened it, we ate some more.

"There isn't much left," I said.

"We were supposed to leave the pudding alone," Huey said.

"We'd better get away from here," I said. We ran into our bedroom and crawled under the bed. After a long time we heard my father's voice.

"Come into the kitchen, dear," he said. "I have something for you."

"Why, what is it?" my mother said, out in the kitchen.

Under the bed, Huey and I pressed ourselves to the wall.

"Look," said my father, out in the kitchen. "A wonderful pudding."

"Where is the pudding?" my mother said.

"WHERE ARE YOU BOYS?" my father said. His voice went through every crack and corner of the house.

We felt like two leaves in a storm.

"WHERE ARE YOU? I SAID!" My father's voice was booming.

Huey whispered to me, "I'm scared."

We heard my father walking slowly through the rooms.

"Huey!" he called. "Julian!"

We could see his feet. He was coming into our room.

He lifted the bedspread. There was his face, and his eyes like black lightning. He grabbed us by the legs and pulled. "STAND UP!" he said.

We stood.

"What do you have to tell me?"

"We went outside," Huey said, "and when we came back, the pudding was gone!"

"Then why were you hiding under the bed?" my father said.

We didn't say anything. We looked at the floor.

"I can tell you one thing," he said. "There is going to be some beating here now! There is going to be some whipping!"

The curtains at the window were shaking. Huey was holding my hand.

"Go into the kitchen!" my father said. "Right now!"

We went into the kitchen.

"Come here, Huey!" my father said.

Huey walked towards him, his hands behind his back.

"See these eggs?" my father said. He cracked them and put the yolks in a pan and set the pan on the counter. He stood a chair by the counter. "Stand up here," he said to Huey.

Huey stood on the chair by the counter.

"Now it's time for your beating!" my father said.

Huey started to cry. His tears fell in with the egg yolks.

"Take this!" my father said. My father handed him the egg beater. "Now beat those eggs," he said. "I want this to be a good beating!"

"Oh!" Huey said. He stopped crying. And he beat the egg yolks.

"Now you, Julian, stand here!" my father said.

I stood on a chair by the table.

"I hope you're ready for your whipping!"

I didn't answer. I was afraid to say yes or no.

"Here!" he said, and he set the egg whites in front of me. "I want these whipped, and whipped well!"

"Yes, sir!" I said, and started whipping.

My father watched us. My mother came into the kitchen and watched us.

After a while Huey said, "This is hard work."

"That's too bad," my father said. "Your beating's not done!" And he added sugar and cream and lemon juice to Huey's pan and put the pan on the stove. And Huey went on beating.

"My arm hurts from whipping," I said.

"That's too bad," my father said. "Your whipping's not done."

So I whipped and whipped, and Huey beat and beat.

"Hold that beater in the air, Huey!" my father said.

Huey held it in the air.

"See!" my father said. "A good pudding stays on the beater. It's thick enough now. Your beating's done." Then he turned to me. "Let's see those egg whites, Julian!" he said. They were puffed up and fluffy. "Congratulations, Julian!" he said. "Your whipping's done."

He mixed the egg whites into the pudding himself. Then he passed the pudding to my mother.

"A wonderful pudding," she said. "Would you like some, boys?"

"No thank you," we said.

She picked up a spoon. "Why, this tastes like a whole raft of lemons," she said. "This tastes like a night on the sea."

Catalogue Cats

"Would you boys like to plant gardens?" my father said.

"Yes," we said.

"Good!" said my father. "I'll order a catalogue."

So it was settled. But afterwards, Huey said to me, "What's a catalogue?"

"A catalogue," I said, "is where cats come from. It's a big book full of pictures of hundreds and hundreds of cats. And when you open it up, all the cats jump out and start running around."

"I don't believe you," Huey said.

"It's true," I said.

"But why would Dad be sending for that catalogue cat book?"

"The cats help with the garden," I said.

"I don't believe you," Huey said.

"It's true," I said. "You open the catalogue, and the cats jump out. Then they run outside and work in the garden. White cats dig up the ground with their claws. Black cats brush the ground smooth with their tails. Yellow and brown cats roll on the seeds to push them underground so they can grow."

"I don't believe you," Huey said. "Cats don't act like that."

"Of course," I said, "*ordinary* cats don't act like that. That's why you have to get them specially – catalogue cats."

15

"Really?" Huey said.

"Really!" I said.

"I'm going to ask Dad about it," Huey said.

"You ask Dad about everything," I said. "Don't you think it's time you learned something on your own for a change?"

Huey looked hurt. "I do learn things by myself," he said. "I wonder when the catalogue will come."

"Soon," I said.

The next morning Huey woke me up. "I dreamed about the catalogue cats!" he said. "Only in my dream the yellow and brown ones were washing the windows and painting the house! You don't suppose they could do that, do you?!"

"No, they can't do that, Huey," I said. "They don't have a way to hold rags and paintbrushes."

"I suppose not," Huey said.

Every day Huey asked my father if the catalogue had come.

"Not yet," my father kept saying. He was very pleased that Huey was so interested in the garden.

Huey dreamed about the catalogue cats again. A whole team of them was carrying a giant pumpkin to the house. One had his teeth around the stem. The others were pushing it with their shoulders and their heads.

"Do you think that's what they really do, Julian?" Huey said.

"Yes, they do that," I said.

Two weeks went by.

"Well, Huey and Julian," my father said, "today is the big day. The catalogue is here."

"The catalogue is here! The catalogue is here! The catalogue is here!" Huey said. He was dancing and twirling around.

I was thinking about going somewhere else.

"What's the matter, Julian?" my father said. "Don't you want to see the catalogue?"

"Oh, yes, I – want to see it,' I said.

My father had the catalogue under his arm. The three of us sat down on the couch.

"Open it!" Huey said.

My father opened the catalogue.

Inside were bright pictures of flowers and vegetables. The catalogue company would send you the seeds, and you could grow the flowers and vegetables.

Huey started turning the pages faster and faster. "Where are the cats? Where are the cats?" he kept saying.

"What cats?" my father said. Huey started to cry.

My father looked at me. "Julian," he said, "please tell me what is going on."

"Huey thought catalogues were books with cats in them. Catalogue cats," I said.

Huey sobbed. "Julian told me! Special cats – cats that work in gardens! White ones – they dig up the dirt. Black ones – they brush the ground with their tails. Yellow and brown ones – they roll on the seeds." Huey was crying harder than ever.

"Julian!" said my father.

"Yes," I said. When my father's voice gets

loud, mine gets so small I can only whisper.

"Julian," my father said, "didn't you tell Huey that catalogue cats are invisible?"

"No," I said.

"Julian told me they jumped out of catalogues! He said they jump out and work in gardens. As soon as you get the catalogue, they go to work."

"Well," said my father, "that's very ignorant. Julian has never had a garden before in his life. I wouldn't trust a person who has never had a garden in his life to tell me about catalogue cats. Would you?"

"No," Huey said slowly. He was still crying a little.

My father pulled out his handkerchief and gave it to Huey. "Now, blow your nose and listen to me," my father said.

Huey blew his nose and sat up straight on the couch. I sat back and tried to be as small as I could.

"First of all," said my father, "a lot of people have wasted a lot of time trying to see catalogue cats. It's a waste of time because catalogue cats are the fastest animals alive. No one is as quick as a catalogue cat. It may be that they really *are* visible and that they just move so quickly you can't see them. But you can feel them. When you look for a catalogue cat over your right shoulder, you can feel

that he is climbing the tree above your left ear. When you turn fast and look at the tree, you can feel that he has jumped out and landed behind your back. And then sometimes you feel all the little hairs on your backbone quiver — that's when you know a catalogue cat is laughing at you and telling you that you are wasting your time.

"Catalogue cats love gardens, and they love to work in gardens. However, they will only do half the work. If they are in a garden where people don't do any work, the catalogue cats will not do any work either. But if they are in a garden where people work hard, all the work will go twice as fast because of the catalogue cats."

"When you were a boy and had a garden," Huey said, "did your garden have catalogue cats?"

"Yes," my father said, "my garden had catalogue cats."

"And were they your friends?" Huey said.

"Well," my father said, "they like people, but they move too fast to make friends.

"There's one more thing," my father said. "Catalogue cats aren't *in* garden catalogues, and no one can order catalogue cats. Catalogue cats are only *around* the companies the catalogues come from. You don't order them, you request them."

"I can write up a request," I said.

"Huey can do that very well, I'm sure," my father said, "if he would like to. Would you like to, Huey?"

Huey said he would.

My father got a piece of paper and a pencil.

And Huey wrote it all down:

REQUESTED:
1 dozen Catalogue Cats
all varieties
WHOEVER
wants to Come
is welCome

Our Garden

We planted tomatoes, marrows, onions, garlic, peas, pumpkins and potatoes. Besides that we planted two special things we saw in the catalogue, which were:

Genuine corn of the Ancients! This sweetcorn grows twenty feet high. Harvest it with a ladder. Surprise your friends and neighbours.

and

Make a house of flowers. Our beans grow

ten feet tall. Grow them around string!
Make a beautiful roof and walls out of their
scarlet blossoms.

Huey was the one who wanted the house of flowers the most. I wanted the giant sweetcorn. My father said he wasn't sure he wanted either giant sweetcorn or a flower house, and if we wanted them we would have to take care of them all summer by pulling up weeds. We said we would.

We planted everything one Saturday. We worked all day long, getting the ground smooth and even, and laying the little seeds down in rows. The whole time I felt the catalogue cats were there, swirling their tails in the air.

We finished just before the sun went down.

My mother gave Huey and me baths.

She said we were darker than the garden. She said we were dirty enough that she could grow plants on our hands and knees.

When we were clean, we had supper, with chocolate pie for dessert, and went to bed.

Huey went to sleep right away. But I didn't.

I put my jacket on over my pyjamas and went out the back door to the garden.

In the dark it looked as if the garden was sleeping. I lay down on the grass. It was cold and a little wet.

I looked up. I thought all the catalogue cats were sitting on the roof of the garage, staring at me. Over the top of the garage was the moon, a little moon with sharp horns. There were birds rustling in the dark branches of the trees.

The seeds were dreaming, I thought. I put my mouth next to the ground, and I spoke to the seeds very softly: "Grow! And you corn seeds, grow high as the house!"

In just one week the seeds did start to grow, and we watered them and weeded them. By the end of the summer we had vegetables from the garden every night. And the sweetcorn did grow as high as the house, although there wasn't very much of it, and it was almost too tough to eat. The best thing of all was Huey's house made of flowers. After a while the flowers dropped their petals and turned into beans, and we ate the beans for supper. So what Huey made was probably the first house anyone ever played in and then ate. Catalogue cats are strange – but a house you can eat for dinner is stranger yet.

Because of Figs

In the summer I like to lie in the grass and look at clouds and eat figs. Figs are soft and purple and delicious. Their juice runs all over my face, and I eat them till I'm so full I can't eat any more.

Because of figs I got a strange birthday present, and because of that birthday present I had some trouble. This is what happened.

It all started a long time ago when I had my fourth birthday. My father came home from work and said, "I have something for you, Julian! Go and look in the car."

I ran to look, and Huey ran after me, tripping on his shoelaces.

When we looked on the back seat of the car, there was a tree! A small tree with just a few leaves.

We ran back to my father. "A tree for a birthday present!" I said.

"A tree for a birthday present!" Huey said. He was two years old, and he always repeated everything I said.

"It's a fig tree," my father told me. "It will grow as fast as you grow, Julian, and in a few years it will have figs that you can pick and eat."

I could hardly wait to grow my own sweet juicy purple figs. We planted the tree by our back fence, and I gave it water every day. And then one morning it had two new leaves.

"Fig tree, you're growing!" I said. I thought I should be growing too. There is a mark on the wall in the bathroom of our house, where my father measures us, and I ran into the house to measure myself against my old mark. I pressed my hand against my head, flat to the wall, and checked where my hand was compared to the old mark. I wasn't any taller.

I walked outside to the fig tree. "I'm not any taller," I said. I touched the fig tree's new leaves. "I want to grow, too!" I said. "You know how to grow, and I don't!" I told the fig tree.

The fig tree didn't say a word.

"Maybe what makes you grow will make me grow," I told it. And very quickly, I picked the fig tree's new leaves and ate them. They tasted worse than spinach. I was pretty sure they would make me grow.

I did a little growing dance around the fig tree, with my hands raised high in the air.

It worked. I stayed taller than Huey. I got taller than my fig tree. And every time my fig tree got new leaves, I saw them and ate them secretly. And when nobody was looking, I did a growing dance.

"If you don't like this, fig tree, just tell me," I'd say.

The fig tree never said a word.

After a year my father looked at my fig tree. "It's a nice little tree," he said, "but it isn't growing." And he started putting fertilizer on my tree, and he looked at it more often.

But when new leaves showed, I saw them first. And I wanted to get taller, so I ate them.

Another whole year went by.

My mark on the bathroom wall went up three inches. I was four inches taller than Huey, and my arm muscle was twice as big as his.

The fig tree hadn't grown at all.

"Fig tree," I said when I took its new leaves, "I'm sorry, but I want to grow tall."

And the fig tree didn't say a word.

One day my father was in the garden.

He walked over to my fig tree. "Julian," he said, "something is the matter with your tree. It hasn't grown. It hasn't grown at all."

"Really?" I said. I didn't look at my father. I didn't look at my fig tree either.

"Do you have any idea what could be wrong?" my father asked.

I looked straight at my feet. I crossed my toes inside my shoes. "Oh, no."

"I think that tree's just plain no good.

We'll pull it out of the ground and get another one."

"Oh no! Don't do that!" I begged.

"Julian," my father said, "do you know something about this tree that I don't know?"

I didn't say anything. And I was glad, very glad, that the fig tree didn't say a word. Finally I said, "It's my tree. Give it one more chance."

"No use waiting around!" my father said. His hand was around the trunk of my tree.

"Please!" I said.

My father's hand relaxed. "After all, it *is* your tree," he said. "Just tell me when you want another one."

All afternoon I couldn't think of anything but all the little fig leaves I'd eaten. I was pretty sure I knew why the fig tree didn't grow.

At bedtime I couldn't sleep, and when Huey went to sleep, I got up and sneaked outside to my fig tree. I told God I knew that the fig leaves belonged to the fig tree. I told the fig tree I was sorry, and I promised I would never eat its leaves again.

The fig tree didn't say a word – but the next week it got two new leaves, and kept them. That night I went to bed happy, and I dreamed a good dream. My fig tree was higher than the house, I was almost as tall as my dad, and there were big figs, juicy figs, sweet figs, falling all over the lawn.

My
Very Strange
Teeth

My mother and Huey were listening. My
father and I were talking.

"Well," my father said, "if you wait long
enough, it will fall out." He was talking
about my tooth, my right bottom front
tooth.

"How long do I have to wait?" I asked.
Because I had *two* right bottom front teeth
– one firm little new one pushing in, and
one wiggly old one.

"I can't say," my father said. "Maybe a
month, maybe two months. Maybe less."

"I don't want to wait," I said. "I want

40

one tooth there, and I don't want to wait two months!"

"All right!" said my father. "I'll take care of it!" He jumped out of his chair and ran out of the door to the garage. He was back in a minute, carrying something – a pair of pliers!

"Your tooth is a little loose already," my father said. "So I'll just put the pliers in your mouth for a second, twist, and the tooth will come out. You won't feel a thing!"

"I won't feel a thing?" I looked at the pliers – huge, black-handled pliers with a long pointed tip. I thought I *would* feel a thing. I thought it would hurt.

"Shall I?" said my dad. He raised the pliers towards my mouth.

"NO!" I said. "Not that way! Don't you know any other way to take out a tooth?"

"Well," he answered, "when I was a boy the main way was with a pair of pliers – but there was another way. Just you wait."

He jumped up again and ran to the cupboard. When he came back, he had a spool of black thread. Thread didn't look as painful as pliers.

"This is a simple way," my father said. "Just let me tie this thread around your old tooth."

"All right," I said.

Very carefully my father tied the end

of the thread around my old tooth. That
didn't hurt.

"Now," my father said, "stand here by
the door."

I stood by the kitchen door, and my
father tied the other end of the thread to
the doorknob.

"Now what?" I said.

"Now," my father said, "you just close
your eyes . . ."

"What are you going to do?" I asked. I wasn't going to close my eyes when I didn't know what was happening.

"This is a *good* method from the old days," my father said. "You close your eyes. Then – very suddenly – I shove the kitchen door shut. Snap! The thread pulls the tooth right out!"

I looked at the kitchen door. It was a lot bigger than I was – and about twenty million times bigger than my tooth.

"Won't it . . . hurt?" I was really afraid I might lose my whole head with the tooth.

"Oh, just a little," my father said. "Just for a *second*."

"No thanks," I said. "Please take this thread off my tooth!"

"All right then." My father shrugged his shoulders and took the string off my tooth.

"Don't you know *any other* way?"

"There is one other way," my father said. "Go into the bathroom, stand over the sink, and just keep pushing the tooth with your finger till it comes out."

"Will that hurt?"

"You can stop pushing when it hurts," my father said. "Of course it takes longer – I would be very glad to do it with either the pliers or the doorknob."

"No thanks," I said. I started pushing on my tooth with my finger. "Why can't I push it out here?" I asked. "Why do I have to do it over the sink?"

"When you get the tooth out," my father said, "it'll bleed. That's why you take the tooth out over the sink – so you have cold water to rinse your mouth and stop the bleeding."

"*How much* bleeding?"

"Some. Enough so you should use the sink."

I decided right then that my old tooth could stay in my mouth right beside the new one as long as it wanted – two months, two years, any time.

"I've changed my mind," I said. "That tooth can stay, even if it is stupid to have two teeth where one should be."

"It's not stupid," my mother said, "just unusual. You have very special teeth. I bet prehistoric cavemen would have liked to have your teeth."

"Why?"

"They ate a lot of raw meat," my mother said. "It must have been hard for a cave boy to eat raw meat with teeth missing. But you have two teeth in the space of one. You could have eaten mastodon meat or sabre-toothed tiger meat, or anything the hunters brought home."

A cave boy with two teeth in place of one. I wished I had a time machine to go back to the *very* old days – before pliers and before doorknobs – back to the caves. I curled my lower lip under.

"You look like a cave boy," my mother said.

"You should show the kids at school your teeth," Huey said.

"Maybe I will," I said.

I went to my room and made a sign for myself. It read:

```
See Cave-Boy Teeth
      Ten pence
  10p          10p
```

I wore the sign at break the next day.

My friends came round. "What does *that* mean?" they asked.

"Uh. Uh." I grunted and held up ten

47

pence. I couldn't explain. If I talked, they'd see my teeth for free.

After a while one girl gave me ten pence, and I showed her my special cave-boy teeth. Some of the other kids had missing teeth, but nobody had two teeth in one space like mine.

I ran all the way home after school to tell my mother what had happened. I said, "Tomorrow I'll show more kids!"

I picked up an apple that lay on the kitchen table and took a big bite.

"Ow!" I said, because I could feel my old tooth twist in my mouth. In a minute, without too much blood, it was lying on my hand. "OW!" I said again, not because it hurt, but because right then was the end of my special, mastodon-eating, double-biting, cave-boy teeth.

Gloria
Who Might Be
My Best Friend

If you have a girl for a friend, people find out and tease you. That's why I didn't want a girl for a friend – not until this summer, when I met Gloria.

It happened one afternoon when I was walking down the street by myself. My mother was visiting a friend of hers, and Huey was visiting a friend of his. Huey's friend is five and so I think he is too young to play with. And there aren't any kids just my age. I was walking down the street feeling lonely.

Near our house I saw a removal van in

front of a brown house,
and men were carrying
in chairs and tables and
bookcases and boxes full
of I don't know what. I
watched for a while, and
suddenly I heard a voice right behind me.

"Who are you?"

I turned round and there was a girl in a
yellow dress. She looked the same age as
me. She had curly hair that was braided
into two pigtails with red ribbons at the
ends.

"I'm Julian," I said. "Who are you?"

"I'm Gloria," she said. "I come from
Newport. Do you know where Newport
is?"

I wasn't sure, but I didn't tell Gloria.
"It's a town by the sea," I said.

"Right," Gloria said. "Can you turn a
cartwheel?"

She turned sideways herself and did two cartwheels on the grass.

I had never tried a cartwheel before, but I tried to copy Gloria. My hands went down in the grass, my feet went up in the air, and – I fell over.

I looked at Gloria to see if she was laughing at me. If she was laughing at me, I was going to go home and forget about her. But she just looked at me very

seriously and said, "It takes practice," and then I liked her.

"I know where there's a bird's nest in your garden," I said.

"Really?" Gloria said. "There weren't any trees in the garden, or any birds, where I lived before."

I showed her where a robin nests and has eggs. Gloria stood up on a branch and looked in. The eggs were small and white. The mother robin squawked at us, and she and the father robin flew around our heads.

"They want us to go away," Gloria said. She got down from the branch, and we went round to the front of the house and watched the removal men carry two rugs and a mirror inside.

"Would you like to come over to my house?" I said.

"All right," Gloria said, "if it is all right with my mother." She ran in the house and asked.

It was all right, so Gloria and I went to my house, and I showed her my room and my games and my rock collection, and then I made strawberry soda and we sat at the kitchen table and drank it.

"You have a red moustache on your mouth," Gloria said.

"You have a red moustache on your mouth, too," I said.

Gloria giggled, and we licked off the moustaches with our tongues.

"I wish you'd live here a long time," I told Gloria.

Gloria said, "I wish I would too."

"I know the best way to make wishes," Gloria said.

"What's that?" I asked.

"First you make a kite. Do you know how to make one?"

"Yes," I said. "I know how." I know how to make good kites because my father taught me. We make them out of two crossed sticks and folded paper.

"All right," Gloria said, "that's the first part of making wishes that come true. So let's make a kite."

We went out into the garage and spread out sticks and newspaper and made a kite.

I fastened on the kite string and went to the cupboard and got rags for the tail.

"Do you have some paper and two pencils?" Gloria asked. "Because now we make the wishes."

I didn't know what she was planning, but I went in the house and got pencils and paper.

"All right," Gloria said. "Every wish you want to have come true you write on a long thin piece of paper. You don't tell me your wishes, and I don't tell you mine. If you tell, your wishes don't come true. Also, if you look at the other person's wishes, your wishes don't come true."

Gloria sat down on the garage floor again and started writing her wishes. I wanted to see what they were – but I went to the other side of the garage and wrote my own wishes instead.

I wrote:

1. I wish I could see the catalogue cats.

2. I wish the fig tree would be the tallest in town.

3. I wish I'd be a great football player.

4. I wish I could ride in an aeroplane.

5. I wish Gloria would stay here and be my best friend.

I folded my five wishes in my fist and went over to Gloria.

"How many wishes did you make?" Gloria asked.

"Five," I said. "How many did you make?"

"Two," Gloria said.

I wondered what they were.

"Now we put the wishes on the tail of the kite," Gloria said. "Every time we tie one piece of rag on the tail, we fasten a wish in the knot. You can put yours in first."

I fastened mine in, and then Gloria fastened in hers, and we carried the kite into the yard.

"You hold the tail," I told Gloria, "and I'll pull."

We ran through the back yard with the kite, passed the garden and the fig tree, and went into the open field beyond our garden.

The kite started to rise. The tail jerked heavily like a long white snake. In a minute the kite passed the roof of my house and was climbing towards the sun.

We stood in the open field, looking up at it. I was wishing I would get my wishes.

"I know it's going to work!" Gloria said.

"How do you know?"

"When we take the kite down," Gloria told me, "there shouldn't be one wish in the tail. When the wind takes all your wishes, that's when you know it's going to work."

The kite stayed up for a long time. We both held the string. The kite looked like a tiny black spot in the sun, and my neck got stiff from looking at it.

"Shall we pull it in?" I asked.

"All right," Gloria said.

We drew the string in more and more until, like a tired bird, the kite fell at our feet.

We looked at the tail. All our wishes were gone. Probably they were still flying higher and higher in the wind.

Maybe I would see the catalogue cats and get to be a good football player and have a ride in an aeroplane and the tallest fig tree in town. And Gloria would be my best friend.

"Gloria," I said, "did you wish we would be friends?"

"You're not supposed to ask me that!" Gloria said.

"I'm sorry," I answered. But inside I was smiling. I guessed one thing Gloria wished for. I was pretty sure we would be friends.

About the Author

Ann Cameron has worked in publishing and as a university teacher. Her most adventurous experience was working with archaeologists on a Mayan dig in the rainforest of Belize. She washed pieces of ancient pottery and cooked for the camp. At night she slept in a hammock in an open-air hut, while around her boa constrictors climbed up to the thatched roof to hunt mice.

After spending many years in New York and Guatemala, Central America, she now lives in Portland, Oregon, USA. She is the author of seventeen books, including the timeless series of stories featuring brothers Julian and Huey, and she has been a finalist for the U.S. National Book Award for Young People's Literature. Please visit **anncameronbooks.com** for further information about Ann and her books.

Make Your Own Pudding

Here's how to make a pudding that tastes like
a night on the sea! Always remember
to ask an adult for help.

You will need:

> 6 tablespoons lemon juice
> (squeeze 3 to 5 lemons)
> 4 eggs
> 1 cup sugar
> 1 cup cream
> 1 tablespoon cornflour

1. Carefully separate the yolks of the eggs from
   the whites.

2. Put the egg yolks in a heavy-bottomed pan
   (the heavy bottom will keep the pudding from
   sticking once it is heated) and beat them with
   an electric whisk until they are foamy.

3. Add the sugar very slowly, beating constantly.
   Beat until this mixture is pale yellow and
   thick enough so that if you drop some from

your whisk it leaves a trail for a few seconds before it blends into the rest of the pan.

4. Beat in the lemon juice.

5. In a bowl, whisk the cornflour into the cream until there are no lumps.

6. Now put the pan with the beaten yolks on the hob over a very low heat and slowly add the cream mixture, stirring all the time with a wooden spoon.

7. Keep stirring until the mixture is very thick. Scrape the bottom of the pan with your spoon as you stir, so that the pudding doesn't stick.

8. When the mixture is thick, take it off the hob and let it cool for about seven minutes.

9. In a mixing bowl, beat the egg whites until they are stiff. Then mix them gently into the pudding. To cool the pudding quickly, put it in the freezer.

What makes the pudding fluffy is the air that you have beaten into it. But the air will gradually escape, so make the pudding only an hour or so before you plan to eat it.

A Glorious Counting Game

1. How many cats can you see?

2. How many stars are there?

3. How many plants are growing in the vegetable plot?

4. What vegetables are in Julian's garden?

Turn to the back of the book to see the answers!

Spot the Difference

There are ten differences between these two pictures. Can you find them all?

Turn to the back of the book to see the answers!

Dad's Really Difficult Quiz

1. Where do Julian and Huey hide after they eat all the pudding?

2. How do white catalogue cats help in the garden?

3. What is "genuine corn of the Ancients"?

4. What does Julian's father give Julian for his birthday?

5. How does Julian lose his "cave-boy" tooth?

6. Who is Julian's best friend?

Have you read this
Julian and Huey story?

See the world through a
dog's eyes – and nose!

Tiger loves his Human family, especially his Boy,
Huey. But whenever he tries to speak to them,
all they can hear is **"YERF!"**

Poor Tiger can never get his point across –
even when he has very important things to say.
About eating Dad's socks, chasing squirrels
. . . or saving Fiona the Cat!

Have you read this
Julian and Huey story?

Little fibs can lead to big trouble!

Julian hates bicycles. He thinks they are boring
and stupid . . . and maybe just a little bit scary.
But his best friend, Gloria, has just got a new bike,
and all she wants is to go cycling with him.

Julian needs to think of an excuse, and fast.
Surely anything is better than braving a bicycle.
Even if it means sweeping floors, weeding the
garden and doing chores all summer . . . ?

Answers

A Glorious Counting Game answers:

1) Nine; 2) Sixty-four; 3) Twenty;
4) Corn, potatoes, pumpkins, beans

Spot the Difference answers:

Dad's Really Difficult Quiz answers:

1) Under the bed; 2) They dig up the dirt;
3) Sweetcorn; 4) A fig tree; 5) He bites an apple;
6) Gloria